THE UGLY GREAT GIANT

For Tyler

ORCHARD BOOKS
96 Leonard Street, London EC2A 4XD
Orchard Books Australia
32/45-51 Huntley Street, Alexandria, NSW 2015
ISBN 1 84362 240 8 (hardback)
ISBN 1 84362 241 6 (paperback)
First published in Great Britain in 2003
First paperback publication in 2004
Text © Malachy Doyle 2003
Illustrations © David Lucas 2003
The rights of Malachy Doyle to be identified as the author
and of David Lucas to be identified as the illustrator of this
work have been asserted by them in accordance with the
Copyright, Designs and Patents Act, 1988.
A CIP catalogue record for this book is available
from the British Library.
1 3 5 7 9 10 8 6 4 2 (hardback)
1 3 5 7 9 10 8 6 4 2 (paperback)
Printed in Great Britain

THE UGLY GREAT GIANT

MALACHY DOYLE
Illustrated by David Lucas

ORCHARD BOOKS

Chapter One

NEVER GAMBLE
WITH A GIANT

Sam was an outdoor sort of a boy, and
there was nothing he liked better than
to wander the hills from morning till
night. One day he was sauntering home
in the evening light, singing away to
himself, when the ground began to rock,
the rocks began to roll and he heard an
ear-splitting whistle. Turning around
to see what it was, he nearly jumped
out of his trousers when he saw an

Ugly Great Giant, striding down the hill towards him.

"Are you any good at cards, young fellow?" boomed the enormous creature, causing the trees to shake and the sheep to scatter.

"I am," said Sam, once he'd got over the shock. "I'm very good at cards." For he was a brave sort of a boy as well as an outdoorsy one, and even though he'd never actually met an Ugly Great Giant before, or even really believed that such a thing existed, he was determined not to let the hideous monstrosity know he was afraid.

"Good stuff," replied the giant, rubbing his hands together. "I like a boy with a bit of spirit in him. Sit down on that boulder, then, and we'll have a game."

So the two sat down. The giant pulled out an oversized pack of cards and started to shuffle.

"What'll we play for?" he asked.

"Hmm," said Sam, scratching his chin and thinking. "How about your largest field against mine?"

Well, it was his dad's field, really, but Sam thought his father probably wouldn't mind, given that they were the poorest of poor farmers and their largest field, which was in fact their only field, was likely to be teeny tinchy tiny compared to that of an Ugly Great Giant's.

"It's a deal," said the giant, dealing the cards.

They were about five times as big as any cards Sam had ever seen, which made them very difficult to hold, but he managed to play, nevertheless. For he'd been taught by his father on the long winter nights, and he was good. Very good.

So they played and Sam won. They played a second time and Sam won again. And the Ugly Great Giant, who turned out to be the world's worst loser as well as the world's greatest eyesore, wasn't too pleased. In fact, he was very displeased, and he was not a happy ogre. He humphed and he grumphed, he snarled and he snorted, but in the end he had to accept that he'd been beaten.

He was determined to get his revenge, though. Oh yes.

Sam was over the moon, of course. He ran home, singing and dancing and whooping for joy, to tell his father of the luck he'd had and what an excellent piece of land he'd won.

"Dad! Dad!" he cried, rushing into the farmhouse. "I met this giant, I played him at cards, and I won us his largest field!"

"Well done, boy!" said his father, delighted.

But when his mother found out, she wasn't happy at all. "What if you'd lost, Sam?" she cried. "And what if he'd eaten you?"

Chapter Two

RAISING THE STAKES

The next day, despite his mother's warnings, Sam returned to the same place. And he didn't have long to wait before the ground began to rock, the rocks began to roll, and there in the distance was the Ugly Great Giant, striding over the hill towards him.

"So what'll we play for today?" boomed the dreadful-looking creature.

"You decide this time," answered Sam.

"Right," said the giant, grinning his beastliest grin. "I've five hundred bullocks with golden horns and silver hooves, and I'll wager them against every one of yours."

"Fair enough," said Sam, thinking there's no way his father would mind, for they'd only one cow, and that was a scraggy old thing that tried to kick you every time you went near, and wouldn't give you milk more than once a week.

They played and they played and it was just like before, Sam won and the giant lost, every time. So he humphed and he grumphed, he snarled and he snorted, he roared till the mountains shook and the clouds burst open.

But Sam was determined not to show any fear, so

he stood and he waited till the ugly,
great, noisy thing stopped uprooting
trees and chucking them into the lake.
Till the foul and horrible
monster stopped cursing
and swearing, snarling
and snorting, and went
off and fetched him
his prize.

And then Sam marched home, proudly leading the five hundred handsomest cattle he'd ever seen behind him.

When he arrived home, his father was totally amazed at the sight of the wonderful herd, even more amazed and delighted than he'd been the day before.

"We're rich, boy!" cried he, throwing

his arms around his only son. "Rich beyond our wildest dreams!"

"We may be rich," said his wife, who never did believe in happy endings, "but nothing good ever came out of giants or gambling, and I don't like it. Not one little bit."

And she sent for Old Martha, the wise woman who lived in the woods, to come and tell them what to do.

Martha studied the leaves at the bottom of Sam's cup, she stared at the flame as it flickered in the fire, she traced the lines on the palm of his hand and then she spoke.

"My advice," she said, "if anyone wants to hear it, is to keep this boy well clear of that nasty giant from now on. He's got away with it once, and away with it twice, but it'll be third time unlucky if they meet up again."

But you know what it's like when

you gamble and win, whether it's marbles or money, bullocks or fields. You think you're never going to lose, and so it was with Sam. Nothing could keep him from another game, and away he went the next day, ignoring every warning.

And when he came to the hillside, there was the Ugly Great Giant, twiddling his chubby thumbs.

"Are you playing or what?" said the monstrous ogre, grinning a horrible grin.

"I am," answered Sam, eagerly, "but I've won your land and I've won your bullocks. What else is there to play for?"

"Oh, I can think of something," said the giant, with an even uglier look than before.

"What's that then?" asked Sam.

"YOUR HEAD!" cried the giant.

Sam was stunned into silence. "Well, I'm not so sure about that," he said, backing away.

"What are you worried about?" said the giant, sneering at him. "Isn't my own head a whole lot bigger than yours, and I'm not afraid!"

Sam knew from the look on the giant's face that there'd be no getting away without playing, so he picked up the cards and began to deal.

And so they played for their heads, but just as Old Martha had warned, the boy's luck had turned. Fear had crept in, and everything, but everything, had changed.

The giant won and Sam lost every single hand. His blood ran cold at the thought of the price he'd have to pay, and he looked all around for a way to escape, but saw none.

But the giant didn't want his revenge there and then. Oh no. He wanted to make Sam suffer.

"You've got four days to say goodbye to the world, boy," boomed the ugly, great, horrible thing, grinning triumphantly. "And then you must come to my castle."

Sam went home, with his heart sunk deep inside him, and when his mother and father saw the look that was on their only child, they knew Old Martha was right and that the boy was in trouble. Big trouble.

He walked straight past them, up

to his room, wouldn't speak a word to anyone and in the morning he was gone. Gone to say goodbye to the world.

Chapter Three

YELLOW LILY

He walked and he walked, did poor Sam, till his legs were dropping from under him. Tramping and stamping, with such a black cloud of gloom filling his head that he didn't hear the wind blow and he didn't hear the birds sing.

Late in the evening, he found himself sitting on a rock, looking all around him. He hadn't a clue where he was, but he knew three things. One, he was sad. Two, he was tired. And three, he was ever so hungry.

Somewhere in the distant gloom, Sam saw a small light at the foot of a hill, and he hoped beyond hope that it might mean somewhere to eat and somewhere to sleep and someone to cheer him up.

Following the light, he came to a tiny cottage. Inside was a little old woman sitting by the fire.

"You're welcome to my house, boy," said the woman, as though she was expecting him. "Pull up a chair and I'll get you some food."

She gave him a bowl of stew and made him up a bed by the fire, and when he was leaving the next morning, she handed him a ball of thread.

"I know all about the trouble you're in, boy. So take this with you, if you want to stay alive," she said. "Throw it out in front of you, and follow it all day as it rolls."

Sam thought this was a strange sort of a thing to do, but if there were any chance it might help him keep his head he decided he'd give it a go. So all day long he followed the thread, and at last towards evening he saw a hill in front of him and a light at the foot of it, just as he had the previous night.

He followed the light and found a house, and there inside was an old, old woman, very like the one he'd met before, only older.

"You're welcome to my house, young man," said the old, old woman, not at all surprised to see him. "Sit down by the fire and I'll bring you some food."

So he did, and she did, and she gave him a bed for the night. And when he was ready for his journey the next morning, she gave him a second ball of thread.

"It's my younger sister you were with before," she said, "and tonight you'll be with my older one. Do what she tells you or all will be lost. Now, do you know what to do with this ball of thread?"

"Throw it in front of me and follow it till evening?" asked Sam.

"That's right," said the old, old woman. "It's your only chance."

So Sam did as he was told. He tossed the ball and it rolled ahead of him, up and down, up and down, all the day till nightfall. And there, for the third time, he found a tiny light, a little house and an old, old, old woman, the eldest sister. Just like the others, only older.

She gave him fried eggs and bacon, a warm feather bed, and in the morning over breakfast, she spoke.

"I know all about your journey, young fellow," she croaked. "You've lost your head to the Ugly Great Giant, isn't that so?"

Sam nodded, sadly.

"The giant has a great castle," continued the ancient woman.

"Around the castle are seven hundred iron spikes, and on every spike but one is some poor unfortunate's head. The seven hundredth spike is empty, and nothing can save you from it if you don't take my advice."

"I will, I will," cried Sam, desperately. "Just tell me what to do."

"Listen carefully, then," said the eldest sister. "And I'll tell you how to get to the giant's castle."

"But that's the last place on earth I want to go!" cried Sam. "I thought you'd tell me how to escape him, not how to find him!"

"The more you keep running," said the old woman, "the worse it'll be when he gets you. But if you do as I say, you just might survive."

"All right," said Sam. "Tell me what to do."

"Here's another ball of thread,"

said the woman, handing it to him. "Throw it and follow it, throw it and follow it, till it leads you to the lake of the Ugly Great Giant. There you'll see his young daughter, Yellow Lily, on her way down to swim. Keep your eyes on her and while she's in the water, slip away with her clothes."

Stranger and stranger, thought Sam, but he followed the ball, up the hills and down the valleys, till he came to a lake, where he hid behind a rock and waited. At midday, Yellow Lily came down to the water, took off her clothes and entered the lake. And while she was swimming, Sam slipped out and stole away her clothes, just as he'd been told.

When Yellow Lily went to come out of the water, she noticed they were missing. "How can I go home without a stitch on me?" she cried. "Whoever it is

took my clothes, I'll forgive you if you bring them here. And if you're in any danger, I'll save you!"

Sam found it a bit hard to believe that a naked girl could save him from an Ugly Great Giant, but he knew he had to take any chance going, so he tossed the clothes out from behind the rock, and shut his eyes till she'd dressed.

"Thank you for giving them back," said the girl, when Sam had come out to join her. "I know why you stole them, and I know well the danger you're in. It's to do with my father, isn't it?"

Sam nodded. "I can hardly believe you're the Ugly Great Giant's daughter," he said. "What'll he do when he finds me?"

"My father has a soft bed waiting for you – a deep tank of water to

drown you in!" answered Yellow Lily.
"But don't be afraid. Go into the tank,
hold your breath, and I'll be there to
save you."

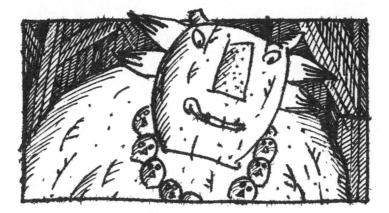

Chapter Four

SHOVELLING MUCK

When the Ugly Great Giant came home that night, the first question he asked was, "Is that boy here yet?"

"I am, sir," said Sam, marching up to him, bold as brass.

"Aha!" said the giant, looking him up and down and licking his lips. "A tasty enough specimen, I'm sure," he said. "Come and get your evening meal, boy. You could do with some meat on your bones!"

"I'll take no food from you, you horrible monster," said Sam. "It won't do me much good, anyway, if you have your evil way."

"That's true enough," replied the giant, with a foul laugh. "Follow me then, and I'll show you to your bed."

He led Sam to a deep tank of water, where he grabbed him by the scruff of the neck and plopped him in. Then, being tired himself from a long day's hunting, the giant lay down on the floor next to the water tank and fell asleep.

The minute her so-called father began to snore, in came Yellow Lily. She helped Sam out of the tank, and gave him food to eat and a safe bed to sleep in.

She watched all night till she heard her father stirring. Then she roused Sam and helped him back into the tank of water.

"Are you still alive in there, boy?" the giant boomed, peering down into the tank.

"I am," said Sam, splashing about.

"Well, you're the strongest swimmer I've ever known," said the enormous bully, trying to hide his disappointment. "Let's get you out of there now, for I've a job for you. I've a stable out here in which I keep sixty horses, and it hasn't been cleaned these two hundred years. When my great-grandmother was a girl, she lost a gold ring in there, and she never could find it. You've got till nightfall to come up with it, and if you don't I'll have your head — on a spike!"

Sam found an old shovel, and he set to work. But there was some sort of magic around, and dark and evil magic it was, because for every shovelful of muck he threw out of the stable, another two shovelfuls came flying back in again.

"How are you getting on, Sam?" came a voice from outside. It was Yellow Lily.

"Not too well, I'm afraid," he answered. "The more of this muck I throw, the more comes in. I'm covered in it, from head to foot, and I haven't a hope of getting the job done in time."

"Yes, you do smell a bit," said Yellow Lily, holding her nose. "But hang on a second and I'll be in there with you."

And she hitched up her skirts, and hopped over the stable door.

She worked like a demon and within an hour and a half, the stable was cleared. And not only that but she held the sparkling ring in her hand, too.

When the Giant came home, his face dropped at the sight of an empty stable. And it dropped even further at the sight of Sam holding his great-grandmother's precious ring.

"It's the devil or my daughter that helped you today, boy," said the giant, in his fury, "for you could never have done it by yourself!"

"It wasn't the devil or your daughter. It was me, all alone," said Sam, crossing his fingers behind his back, and deciding that a little white lie wouldn't go too much against him when his life was at stake.

"Will you have some food with me then?" asked the monster, trying again to get some meat on the bones of the boy.

"I won't," said Sam, "for all I want is sleep."

He went into the tank, as before, washed all the muck off himself, and then as soon as her so-called father was snoozing, Yellow Lily came along and helped him out.

She gave Sam a good supper, a warm bed, and he was back in the water by morning.

Chapter Five

THE NASTY BIT
(Not to be read if you don't like nasty bits.)

"Are you alive at all?" called the giant at daybreak, peering into the bottomless tank.

"I am," said Sam, much to the big fellow's dismay.

"Well, I've great work for you today," said the obnoxious eyesore, not wishing to show his surprise. "That stable you cleared yesterday hasn't been roofed for a hundred years. You're to thatch it by nightfall with the feathers of birds, and no two feathers of the same colour or kind. If you don't, I'll have your puny little head on the seven hundredth spike by morning!"

All he gave Sam was a whistle to call the birds, but it was no use for no matter how hard he blew, none came to him.

Sam's spirits rose, though, when he saw Yellow Lily, coming over the field with food and drink. He set to eating, she set to thatching, and he hadn't finished eating and drinking

before she'd thatched the whole stable
with feathers, and no two of them of
the same colour or kind.

"Have you done as I told you?" boomed the giant when he returned that evening.

"I have," said Sam.

"Then you must have had help from the devil or my daughter!" roared the bloodthirsty tyrant.

"I'd no help from anyone," replied the boy, crossing his fingers once more. And he spent that night as he had the ones before.

The next morning, the giant was disgusted to find Sam fit and well again.

"I've great work for you today, boy," he said, trying to hide his disappointment. "You're to find the tallest tree in the forest. It's nine hundred feet or more, and there's not one single branch on it but a tiny twig at the very top, and resting on that twig there's a crow's nest with one egg. I want that egg for my supper tonight, or you know what you'll get?"

"Head on a spike?" said Sam, grimly.

"Head on a spike!" grinned the giant.

The ugly monster went hunting, and Sam went into the wood to seek out the tree. When he found it, at last, he did his best to shake the egg down from the top, but it wouldn't move. He tried to climb the trunk, but it was as slippery as a fish.

He had a drink from a stream, and sat down. And he was sitting there on a stump with his head in his hands, when up came Yellow Lily.

"Are you saying goodbye to your head?" she joked.

"It's not funny, girl," said Sam. "There's some sort of an egg in the top of that tree, and if I don't fetch it, I'm a goner."

"It's a long way up, right enough," said Yellow Lily, craning her neck. "Sit down and have something to eat while I think about it."

So she sat and she thought. And she sat and she thought. "Now, you might not like this idea much," said she, after a while, "but it's the only way you'll save your head."

"What's that?" asked Sam.

"You've got to kill me," said Yellow Lily, handing him a knife.

"Kill you?" said Sam, horrified.

"Yes, kill me," said Yellow Lily, calmly, as though she was asking him nothing worse than to go down to the shops to buy her a packet of Jelly Babies. "Strip the flesh from my bones, take them apart, and use them as steps for climbing the tree. Then when you're coming down, collect each bone behind you and put them back together. Drape my flesh over them, sprinkle me with water  from this stream, and I'll be alive again and no harm done."

"You've got to be joking!" said Sam. "You can't expect me to do that."

"It's your only chance to stay alive," said the girl. "And I'll be fine, believe me, for I'm not of your kind."

Sam didn't know what to do, but Yellow Lily kept reassuring him. "It'll be all right, I promise. As long as you do exactly as I've told you."

So Sam took his courage in both hands and the knife in another and began to sharpen it on a stone.

"And don't forget to collect every single one of my bones on the way down," warned Yellow Lily, "or you won't be able to put me back together again."

Well it was a bad business, sure enough, but Sam knew by now that Yellow Lily was a magical creature as well as a girl, and so he had to trust her when she said it'd be all right.

So he killed her, though it nearly broke his heart to do so. He cut the flesh from Yellow Lily's bones and took them apart. Then, as he went up, he pushed each bone into the side of the tree ahead of him, just as he'd been told. He used them as steps to climb all the way up to the tiny twig at the very top, with the nest in it.

He picked up the egg that the giant wanted for his breakfast, and he wrapped it up safely in his handkerchief. Then he tucked it deep into his pocket and down he came, gently, gently, so as not to damage the egg, carefully, carefully, putting his foot on every bone.

And when he'd used each bone to climb down, he pulled it out and brought it with him, so that by the time he was almost down he'd gathered up all but the bottom one.

"I've done it!" cried Sam. And with a whoop and a holler he jumped to the ground, lay all Yellow Lily's bones back in the right order by the side of the stream and sprinkled water on them.

Quick as a flash, she rose up before him, just as she'd said she would, but there was a look of terrible sadness on her face.

"Didn't I tell you to collect every one of my bones on the way down?" she cried.

"That's what I did," said Sam.

"You did not!" cried the girl. "You left my little toe on the tree, and now I've only nine!"

Sam dashed back to the tallest tree in the forest and tried to pull out the bottom bone, but it was stuck fast.

"It's no use," said Yellow Lily, sadly, "for now I'm lame. You had to do it then and there for it to work."

Chapter Six

HEAD ON A SPIKE?

When the Ugly Great Giant came home that night, after a long day's hunting, he stormed into the castle, yelling, "Where's that boy? I'm hungry!"

Sam appeared in front of him, looking sheepish, and the giant licked his lips.

"Well, what's for supper?" asked the giant, with an evil grin. "You or the crow's egg?"

Sam cast his eyes down, and the giant thought he had him at last.

"Aha!" cried the hungry horror, licking his lips once more. And his stomach rumbled at the thought of the delightful meal to come. "You won my field and you captured my bullocks, you found the ring and you thatched the stable, but I knew you couldn't beat me on this one!"

Sam reached into his pocket and pulled out his hanky.

"There's no use snivelling, boy," roared the brutal butcher. "You played, you lost, and now you pay!"

He took a step forward, and was just about to grab Sam by the neck when the boy unwrapped the hanky and with a flourish and a smile, revealed the egg.

"No!" cried the foul assassin, gasping for breath. "I don't believe it!"

He fell onto a sofa, which collapsed

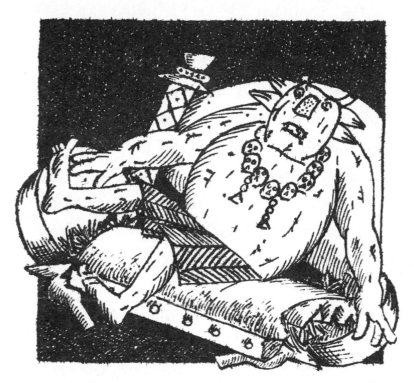

under his weight. "I suppose you'll
have to keep your head a while longer
then," the monster wheezed, as he
picked himself up from the floor. "The
last spike will have to stay empty for
now. But I swear you must have had
the devil or my daughter on your side
to be able to do the things you've done.
Which is it?"

"You're right!" cried Sam, triumphantly, for he'd decided it wouldn't do any harm to tell the truth at last. "Yellow Lily's been helping me all this time. I'm leaving this castle, she's coming away with me, and there's nothing you can do about it, you loathsome monster!"

"So you think you'll escape, do you?" hissed the giant, furiously. "Well you've got another think coming, boy. You've been cheating me, left, right and centre, and you know what I do to cheats?"

Sam didn't hang around to find out. He grabbed Yellow Lily by the hand and together they ran like the wind, up, down and all through the castle. They were small and the giant was big, so they could squeeze through doorways he couldn't fit, and hide in places he couldn't see.

At last they came to the gates, ran across the drawbridge, and were heading off across the open ground towards the woods.

"We're well ahead of him," said Sam, panting. "Once we get to the trees we'll be fine."

"I'm afraid we won't, Sam," said Yellow Lily, stumbling. "For I'm lame without my toe, like I told you, and I can't run a step more."

"Here, climb up on my back," said the boy. He bent down, she jumped up, and Sam ran as fast as he could. But it wasn't fast enough.

"He's at the gates of the castle, coming across the drawbridge!" cried Yellow Lily, looking back. "He'll have us in no time!"

And he would have, too. But what they didn't know was that a trillion and eight tiny woodworm had spent a hundred and thirty-five years, four months and twenty-six days nibbling their way through the great blocks of wood that held the drawbridge in place. It was still strong enough to hold the weight of Sam and Yellow Lily, but when the Ugly Great Giant came bounding across it in a dreadful fury, he was too heavy altogether.

So, with a splitting and shattering, the bridge chose that very moment to collapse into the raging torrents below, taking the hideous man-eater with it.

"Come back!" he yelled, spluttering, as the river carried him away. "I can't swim!"

And do you think Sam went back to save his evil tormentor? He did not. And do you think Yellow Lily went back to rescue her cruel father? She did not. For she'd given up on the Ugly Great Giant and all his nastiness years ago. Father or no father, all she wanted was a bit of peace and quiet, and the chance to live with people who didn't bite your head off as soon as look at you.

So they turned and they ran, Sam and Yellow Lily, and they didn't stop running till they were well into the woods.

"Will you come home with me to my mum and dad?" asked the boy, and Yellow Lily said she'd like that very much.

So off they went, stopping off only to thank the three ancient sisters for their help and to introduce them to the lovely Yellow Lily.

And then, four weeks after he'd left, Sam arrived home.

"My son, my son, my darling son!" cried his father, wrapping his arms around him.

"We'd almost given up on ever seeing you again," cried his weeping mother, for they'd been searching high and low, far and wide.

And when Sam told them all that had happened, and all that Yellow Lily had done to save their beloved boy from the evil clutches of the Ugly Great Giant, they hugged her, too, and asked her if she'd like to stay and be a daughter to them.

And Yellow Lily said yes.

JALOPY

GERALDINE McCAUGHREAN

Illustrated by Ross Collins

JALOPY

BY GERALDINE McCAUGHREAN

Masher and Spug ran out of the bank, chased by ten security guards, two big dogs and the clang of alarm bells. "Quick! Into the car!" cried Masher. But Jalopy was gone.

Mrs Ethel Thomas wins a beautiful shiny red car in a competition and calls the car Jalopy. But Mrs Thomas can't drive, so the car goes nowhere until one day bank-robbers Spug and Masher steal Jalopy to be their get-away car...

An exciting and funny story by a much-loved author.

ORCHARD GREEN APPLES

HARDBACK

☐ Monkey-Man   *Sandra Glover*   1 84362 276 9

☐ The Ugly Great Giant   *Malachy Doyle*   1 84362 240 8

☐ Jalopy   *Geraldine McCaughrean*   1 84362 266 1

☐ Sugar Bag Baby   *Susan Gates*   1 84362 070 7

ALL PRICED AT £8.99

PAPERBACK

☐ Monkey-Man   *Sandra Glover*   1 84362 278 5

☐ The Ugly Great Giant   *Malachy Doyle*   1 84362 241 6

☐ Jalopy   *Geraldine McCaughrean*   1 84362 267 X

☐ Sugar Bag Baby   *Susan Gates*   1 84362 071 5

ALL PRICED AT £3.99

Orchard Green Apples are available from all good bookshops,
or can be ordered direct from the publisher:
Orchard Books, PO BOX 29, Douglas IM99 1BQ
Credit card orders: please telephone 01624 836000 or fax 01624 837033
or visit our Internet site: www.wattspub.co.uk
or e-mail: bookshop@enterprise.net for details.

To order please quote title, author and ISBN
and your full name and address.
Cheques and postal orders should be made payable to 'Bookpost plc.'
Postage and packing is FREE within the UK
(overseas customers should add £1.00 per book).
Prices and availability are subject to change.